Brian
the Smelly Bear

Mark Chambers

 BONNEY PRESS

Published by Bonney Press,
an imprint of Hinkler Books Pty Ltd
45–55 Fairchild Street
Heatherton Victoria 3202 Australia
www.hinkler.com.au

BONNEY
PRESS

Author and illustrator: Mark Chambers
Prepress: Graphic Print Group

ISBN: 978 1 7436 3501 8

Printed and bound in China

Brian is a very smelly bear,

But he doesn't seem to care.

"I smell nice!" he shouts. "I am *clean*!"

His friends, however, are not so keen...

Some cough, some wheeze and hold their noses tight.

His best pals, the rabbits, leap far out of sight.

YUCK!

But Brian doesn't seem to have a clue.
He says, "Mmmm." Others say, "Pooooh!"

He smells out the bushes, he honks out the shed!

His stench would keep spiders away from your bed.

He stinks out the pond and pongs out the wood.

You'd be wise to run far away if you could!

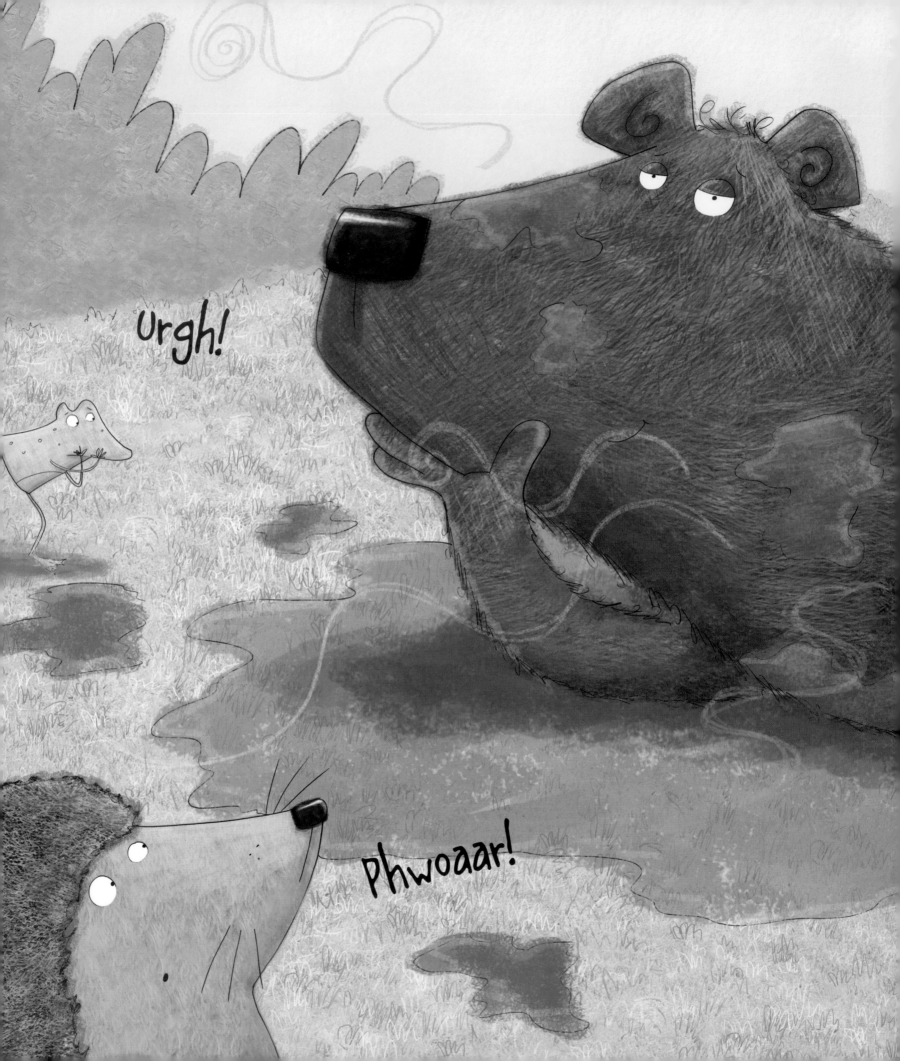

The frogs groan, "Urgh!" The hedgehogs say, "Phwoaar!"

But Brian just rolls in the mud on the floor.

"I smell great," he says. "I don't sniff."

You wouldn't say that if **you** caught a whiff!

One morning, old Badger said, "That's *enough*!
What *are* we to do with that big stinky scruff?"

"We just can't go on. He's putting us to shame.

His smell is so awful, but to him it seems tame."

We agree!

The friends made a plan named "**MISSION: SCRUB**",

And armed themselves with soap and a tub.

"Hey Brian!" they called. "Come on over here!"

Brian looked at them puzzled, scratching his ear.

"We've found an old bath. It's full of mud and it stinks!"

The animals all whispered, "Well, that's what *he* thinks."

Brian grinned as he ran; the ultimate dash.

He leapt high as a kite, then down with a...

SPLAAAASSSSH!!

"This tub isn't full of stinky, smelly stuff!

It's just soapy water," Brian said in a huff.

So Brian, who smelt more than anyone you know,

More than rotten old socks and fluff on your toe...

Now smells just like flowers, and has changed his name,

To just Brian Bear, never smelly again!